Friendship
Fudge

Look out for more

# Bake a Wish

books:

Feel Good Fairy Cakes

Can-Do Crispies

Get-Better Jelly

Feel Fearless Flapjacks

Mend-It Muffins

# Bake a Wish

## Friendship Fudge

Lorna Honeywell

Illustrated by Samantha Chaffey

**SCHOLASTIC**

*With special thanks to Pearl Morrison*

First published in the UK in 2012 by Scholastic Children's Books
An imprint of Scholastic Ltd
Euston House, 24 Eversholt Street
London, NW1 1DB, UK
Registered office: Westfield Road, Southam, Warwickshire, CV47 0RA
SCHOLASTIC and associated logos are trademarks
and/or registered trademarks of Scholastic Inc.

ISBN 978 1 407 13482 6

A CIP catalogue record for this book is
available from the British Library.

Printed and bound by CPI Group (UK) Ltd, Croydon, CR0 4YY
Papers used by Scholastic Children's Books are made from
wood grown in sustainable forests.

1 3 5 7 9 10 8 6 4 2

www.scholastic.co.uk/zone

*For Kitty Morrison, also affectionately known as Granny Orkney.*

# Best Friends

Lily looked up at the big round clock on the classroom wall. Soon the home-time bell would ring, but she still hadn't finished the Halloween mask she was making.

Snip, snip, snip went her scissors as she cut out a big smiley mouth and two eyes. Bits of orange paper fell on to her desk and landed on her books and pencils. Lily's desk was always messy. She tried very hard to keep it tidy but it just seemed to get in a muddle again.

It was in an especially big muddle after she'd made her mask, and there was paper everywhere.

"Time to tidy up, please," Miss Carr, her teacher, said.

Lily made one more snip with her scissors and the pumpkin mask was finished.

Lily put her scissors away in the art cupboard and hurried back to her desk to tidy up the bits of orange paper. As she was dropping them into the bin by the door someone gave an excited yell.

Lily turned round. Stephie, who sat at the desk next to her, was holding up a party invitation. She waved the invitation around for everyone to see. "Antonia's invited me to her Halloween party!"

"I'm going too!" said Flo, who sat just behind Lily.

Lily hurried over to her desk, but there was no envelope waiting for her.

She looked over at Antonia, who was still rushing around the classroom giving out the last of the invitations.

"It's going to be the best Halloween party ever!" Lily heard her say. "We're going to have games and lots of yummy treats to eat."

Antonia had one invitation left in her hand. Lily smiled. *That one must be mine!* she thought. She smiled at Antonia and held out her hand. Antonia grinned back . . . and handed the invite to Sam! Lily couldn't understand it. She was Antonia's best friend! Why hadn't she been asked to the party?

Antonia had invited everyone else.

She looked down to hide how upset she was and quickly pushed her things into her school bag. When Miss Carr let them go, Lily hurried out into the corridor and grabbed her coat from the peg. Everyone around her was talking excitedly about what costumes they would wear to the party and what spooky games they were going to play.

Lily rushed out into the playground without even doing her coat up. Her little brother, Archie, and Grandma were waiting for her in their usual place under the willow tree. Archie was wearing a red woollen hat with a big pom-pom. Grandma had on a thick green winter coat that made her look even more cuddly than usual. Lily ran over to join them.

"Hello, Lily," Grandma said with a big happy smile. "Brrrrr!" she pretended to shiver. "Aren't you cold? Let me help you with your coat."

Lily was doing up the buttons when Antonia walked by.

"Bye, Lily," she said with a smile and a little wave. "See you tomorrow."

Lily turned away as tears sprang to her eyes.

"What's wrong, Lily?" Grandma asked. "Why didn't you say goodbye to Antonia? She looked very upset."

Lily's voice wobbled. "Everyone in the class is invited to her Halloween party except me."

Grandma looked puzzled. "But Lily, we're *all* invited to the party – Mum, Archie, you and me. Antonia's mum phoned today. She asked if we would bake some special Halloween treats to take with us."

"Antonia's *mum* invited us," Lily sobbed. "Antonia doesn't want me to come, or she would have given me an invitation."

"I'm sure there must be some mistake," Grandma said.

Lily shook her head sadly. "Antonia doesn't want to be my best friend any more."

A cold breeze ruffled the branches of the tree, making Archie's teeth chatter.

Grandma put her arms around them both. "Come on," she said, "let's go home where it's nice and warm."

Grandma and Grandpa lived around the corner, and every day Grandma collected them from school and took them to her cosy house to play until Mum and Dad finished work.

As they walked along, Lily felt more
and more unhappy. If she and Antonia
weren't best friends any more, then who
would she sit next to at lunch? Who
would be her partner in PE? Who would
she play with at break time? She was
feeling very lonely until a small hand
took hers. Archie was looking up at her.
"I'm still your friend," he said.

## 2

# A Giant Spider

The next day at school all Lily's class talked about was Antonia's Halloween party. But Antonia and Lily didn't talk to each other at all. The day after that, things got even worse. Antonia had already found a new friend. Her name was Stephie. She had a real charm bracelet with lots of different animals on it that she wore at school even though jewellery wasn't allowed.

Finally it was Saturday – the day of the

party. Lily woke up with such a horrible feeling in her tummy that she couldn't eat her breakfast. Mum was busy rushing around the kitchen packing bags to take to Grandma's house.

"We'll set off straight after breakfast," Mum said. "We'll need plenty of time to do all the baking for Antonia's party."

"Why can't I stay here with Dad?" Lily asked for the fifth time. "I don't want to help cook anything for Antonia's party. I'm not even invited."

Mum sat down at the table next to her. "Lily, darling, you *are* invited," she said. "When Antonia's mum asked us to help at the party, she probably thought there was no need to write an invitation. After all, you and Antonia are best friends."

"No, we're not." Lily looked down at her knees. "Not any more."

Mum gave her a hug. "I'm sure you'll enjoy the party once we get there. I'm just going to put our Halloween costumes in the car."

"I won't need one," Lily told her. "I'm *not* going to the party!"

"OK, if that's what you want." Mum gave her a squeeze. "But at least we can still have a lovely day baking at Grandma's."

Lily nibbled her toast. She and Antonia always did something fun at Halloween. Last year they'd dressed up like witches' cats and gone trick or treating. And the year before that they'd had a sleepover and stayed up really late telling spooky stories. Halloween wasn't

going to be any fun without Antonia.

"Lily! Look at me!" Archie said. He crawled into the kitchen wearing a spider costume Mum had made him. It had lots of sticky-out spider legs made out of old stuffed tights.

"Why are you wearing your costume *now*?" Lily asked. "The party isn't until this afternoon."

"Because it's Halloween!" he said. "I'm going to be a creepy spider all day!" He wiggled his extra legs around to make Lily laugh, but she just sighed and put her head in her hands.

"Can we bake really *scary* treats at Grandma's, Mum?" Archie asked.

Mum smiled. "Grandma says we can choose whatever we like from her recipe books." She poured him a bowl of cereal. "Eat up and then we can set off straight after breakfast."

Archie raced through his cereal and ran to get in the car. "Come on, Lily!" he yelled. Lily followed him slowly as he climbed on to the back seat of the car.

"You're sitting on one of my spider legs," Archie said. Lily moved it, and sighed as another one ended up on her head.

"Off we go!" Mum said, and the car pulled away.

Lily stared out of the window as they drove along. Everywhere she looked she was reminded of Halloween. The baker's shop window was full of orange and purple

spooky cakes. There was a big tub of pumpkins outside the supermarket and the toy shop had bats and black cats hanging on the door.

Everyone was having a lovely Halloween except her.

The car stopped at the traffic lights. "You're very quiet, Lily," Mum said. "What are you thinking?"

"Nothing," Lily mumbled, and went back to staring out of the window.

Archie had been quietly singing a spooky song to himself, but he suddenly stopped and called out, "Look! There's Antonia!" He was pointing to the gift shop across the street. Lily's stomach did a little flip. Antonia was standing outside the shop with Stephie and they were laughing together. Lily gasped as Antonia held something up in the air – a bracelet just like Stephie's.

# 3

## Hector to the Rescue

Grandma's cat, Hector, was sitting up on the gatepost when the car stopped in front of the house. He gave a meow as Lily and Hector climbed out of the car.

"Hello, Hector," Lily said and stroked his furry head.

"Do you like my costume, Hector?" Archie asked, giving a twirl that made his spider legs wave around.

Hector stared at him with big wide eyes. "Meow!" he said and leapt from the gate.

Archie ran up the path after him, calling, "Stop! It's only me!" But Hector raced away across the garden with his little collar bell ringing. He disappeared behind a big pile of leaves Grandpa was raking up for a bonfire. Grandpa was wearing a hat and his big winter jacket and whistling as he worked.

When he saw Archie he pretended to be scared. "Aaagh!" he yelled. "A giant spider!"

Archie laughed and did another twirl. Lily stood on the path staring at Grandpa. "He's not really a spider, you know," she said.

Grandpa walked over and gave Lily a hug. "What costume are you wearing to the party?"

Lily sighed. "I'm not going."

Grandpa looked surprised. "But I thought you liked Halloween parties?"

"Antonia and Lily have fallen out," Archie told Grandpa. "Antonia's new friend is called Stephie."

"Lily! Archie!" Mum called as she carried the bags inside.

Lily felt her bottom lip wobble as Archie rushed into the house. Hector trotted out from behind the pile of leaves and rubbed up against her leg. Lily bent down to stroke his soft ears. "You're my friend, aren't you, Hector," she smiled as they went indoors.

"Meow," Hector agreed.

The kitchen was cosy and warm and smelled of scones and jam. While Archie showed off his spider costume to Grandma, Lily slumped down in Grandpa's comfy chair.

"Are you going to help us bake for Antonia's party?" Grandma asked.

Lily shook her head.

"That's a shame," Grandma said, "because I've found the *perfect* recipe book."

She walked over to the large dresser and chose a book from a jam-packed shelf.

"This is the one," she said. "*Spooky Recipes for Halloween!*"

Grandma set it down on the table

and Mum and Archie gathered around as she flicked through the pages. Lily sat watching them from the corner.

"Can we make *all* the recipes?" Archie asked.

Grandma laughed. "We won't have time to make them all. I think we should choose two."

"How about Meringue Ghosts?" Mum asked.

"Yes!" Archie said. He pointed to a picture on the book cover. "And Creepy Cookies!"

"What's the first thing we do before we start baking?" Grandma asked.

"Wash our hands!" Archie said and ran to the kitchen sink.

Lily watched as Mum got bowls out of the cupboard and Grandma put the scales down on the table. Archie had finished washing his hands and was trying to put on his dinosaur apron, but his spider legs kept getting in the way.

Mum and Grandma laughed. "You've got too many legs!" Mum said as she squeezed and twisted the spider legs to fit around the apron.

At last Archie was ready.

Grandma looked at Lily slouched in the chair.

"Why don't you come along to the party and see if you can make up with Antonia?"

Lily looked at the floor. "She doesn't want to be my friend. And I don't even know why!" she finished with a sob.

Grandma gently squeezed her hand. "I think you should talk to her. That way you'll find out."

Just then the phone started to ring in the hall. Grandma hurried away to answer it while Mum borrowed one of Grandma's aprons. She had chosen the stripy rainbow one with big patched pockets. Lily could see her own apron hanging on the back of the kitchen door.

"I'll start making the Meringue Ghosts," Mum was telling Archie. "They only need sugar and eggs. Can you help Grandma with the cookies? They need lots of mixing and stirring."

Archie nodded excitedly. "I like mixing and stirring."

Lily hated feeling so miserable when Archie and Mum were having fun.

As if he knew she was feeling bad, Hector jumped up on Lily's lap and started purring loudly.

"I'm feeling very fed up," Lily whispered in Hector's ear. "I wish I could think of a way to be best friends with Antonia, like I was before. But I don't know how."

She went to tickle Hector's chin but he leapt back down to the floor. She watched him trot across the kitchen with his little collar bell ringing. He stopped right in front of Grandma's sideboard. "Meow," he said and stared up at a stripy yellow jar on the top shelf.

Lily gasped. Grandma's magic jar! It had helped make Archie's sore throat better and it had given her courage to sing in the Easter Show at school. Maybe

it would help her to be friends with
Antonia.

"Great idea, Hector!" She sat up
straight in her chair just as Grandma
walked back into the kitchen.

"Grandma!" Lily said. She was suddenly
very excited. "Hector's given me an idea!
I know how to make Antonia my friend
again!"

# 4

## A Very Important Recipe

"What's your idea, Lily?" Archie asked.

Lily pointed to the yellow and white striped jar on the top shelf of the dresser. "I can make a wish on Grandma's magic cooking jar!"

Grandma smiled. "I think that's a very good idea."

"The jar makes wishes come true," Archie whispered to Mum. "But it's a secret."

"Don't worry," she whispered back. "I won't tell anyone."

Grandma carried the jar over to the table and set it down.

Lily touched it with her fingertips, closed her eyes and made her wish. *Please help me to make friends with Antonia.*

She opened her eyes. Archie was now standing on the chair next to her. "Look inside!" he urged.

Lily lifted the lid and put her hand into the jar. "Oh!" she said, and brought out a tin. She read the label. "Condensed milk. What's that?"

"It's very thick, sweetened milk," Mum said. "Perfect for baking."

"What else is there?" Archie asked. "Can you see chocolate?"

"Yes!" Lily pulled out a bar of chocolate. "That's it," she told Archie.

All that was left inside the jar was a white piece of paper.

"That's the magic recipe," Archie told Mum.

Lily handed the recipe to Grandma. The magic recipes never had a name but Grandma always seemed to know exactly what they were for.

"This is a very important recipe," Grandma announced. She looked at Lily and smiled. "It's for Friendship Fudge!"

Lily felt happier already. "Friendship Fudge! Will it make me and Antonia friends again?" she asked.

"I'm sure it will," Grandma said. "If you both really want it to." Then she added, "It takes two people to make a friendship."

"I know!" Lily said. She took a deep breath. "I'm going to talk to her."

"Does that mean you're coming to the party?" Archie asked.

"Yes," said Lily. "I'm going to give the Friendship Fudge to Antonia." She looked at Grandma. "Will you help me make it?"

"Of course I'll help," Grandma said.

Lily gave an excited smile. "It really will be Friendship Fudge because I'll make it *especially* for Antonia."

"Then let's get started!" Grandma said. "We have lots to do before the party!"

Lily quickly washed her hands and put on her yellow apron with the cupcake pockets. Hector jumped up on the chair next to her at the table.

Lily started by reading the Friendship Fudge recipe. She only needed four ingredients: the chocolate and condensed milk that she had found inside the jar, as well as butter and icing sugar. The butter was already on the table, and there was only one place the icing sugar would be – the Yummy Cupboard. That was where Grandma kept all her baking ingredients and it was one of Lily's favourite places in the whole entire world. Inside the little room there were wooden shelves that stretched all

the way up to the ceiling, all of them full of packets and boxes and bottles and brightly coloured cake decorations.

The cupboard always smelled delicious, too. Today it had a lovely Halloween smell of sticky toffee apples and melted marshmallows. Lily was taking a big sniff when Archie came hurrying in. "I have to find the biscuit cutters!" he gasped. "Grandma says they're in a box on the shelf!"

He crouched down to take a closer look.

"There they are!" Lily said. She pointed to an old plastic ice cream tub with the words COOKIE CUTTERS written on it in big letters. Lily watched Archie open the lid and look inside.

"Ooooh!" he said. There were lots of differently shaped cookie cutters inside. Lily grinned as Archie pulled out a teddy bear shape, lots of different-sized hearts, and even a Christmas tree. "I need Halloween shapes," he said. He searched around in the box. "Here they are!" he smiled, bringing out cutters shaped like a pumpkin and a witch's hat and a bat.

Lily would have loved to use them, too. They looked so much fun. But her recipe was more important. It was going to make her friends with Antonia again.

"I'm going to make Creepy Cookies!" Archie

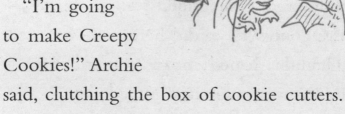

said, clutching the box of cookie cutters.

He hurried out of the Yummy Cupboard and disappeared behind the open door, his spider legs waving goodbye to Lily.

Lily picked up the bag of icing sugar. She took one last look around the Yummy Cupboard. "I'm going to need extra-special magic today," she said. And that's when she saw a small red box tucked into the corner of a shelf. Lily picked it up and hurried out into the kitchen.

"Grandma?" she said. "Can I use this box to put the Friendship Fudge in?"

"Of course," Grandma said. "And we can make it extra pretty by putting a piece of ribbon around it too."

Lily smiled. She could feel the magic starting to work already.

Grandma set out a saucepan and a wooden spoon for her.

"The first thing you need to do is break up the chocolate and put it in a pan," Grandma explained. "Then pour in the condensed milk and the butter, and I'll melt it all together on the cooker."

Lily thought that sounded fun, so she set to work breaking the chocolate into squares.

Archie tugged on Grandma's sleeve. "Can we make the Creepy Cookies now?"

"Yes," Grandma said. "Let's get started."

Suddenly the kitchen was a whirl of activity! Grandma and Archie began measuring out flour, sugar, vanilla extract, eggs, butter and baking soda. Lily waited patiently until they'd finished with the scales, then carefully weighed out her butter.

Mum started breaking eggs into a bowl to make her Meringue Ghosts.

Hector sat quietly, watching and purring loudly as Archie sieved flour and Grandma

started beating butter, egg and vanilla extract together in a bowl.

"How are you getting on, Lily?" Mum asked. "Do you need any help?"

"Yes, please," Lily smiled. "Can you open the tin of milk?"

"Of course," Mum said. "It's nice to see you smiling again." Mum passed Lily the open can and kissed her on the top of her head.

Lily poured the condensed milk into the pan on top of the butter and chocolate. "Done!" she said happily. "Grandma, can you melt this for me now?" she asked.

"Of course," Grandma smiled as she put the pan on the hob.

Lily climbed on a chair to watch as Grandma stirred and stirred. The kitchen filled with the delicious smell of melted chocolate. Soon the mixture was smooth and thick.

"What's next?" Grandma asked.

Lily looked again at the recipe. "I have to weigh out the icing sugar now."

But Archie was using the scales to weigh out sugar for his cookie mixture. While Lily waited her turn, she watched Mum break open an egg against the side of the bowl. She poured the egg out of the shell into her palm.

"I just need the white part of the egg for my meringues," Mum said. Lily watched as Mum let the white runny part of the egg drip down through her fingers into the bowl. The round yellow part was left in her hand. "It's called the yolk," Mum told her and plopped it into a cup.

"What happens to the yolks now?" Lily asked. "Do you put them in the bin?"

"Oh, no," Grandma said. "I'll store them in the fridge, ready to make some custard. We can't waste any of the nice eggs that Jessie and Bessie laid for us."

Lily grinned as she thought about Grandma's chickens, then watched as

Mum quickly whisked all the egg whites in the bowl using an electric whisk. In no time at all the eggs went from being slippery and clear to white and fluffy like clouds. Round and round went Mum's whisk until the eggs turned into white shiny mountains.

"It's like magic!" Archie said. Lily nodded in amazement. She couldn't believe an egg could do that!

"Don't you have some baking magic to do as well, Lily?" Grandma asked with a twinkle in her eye.

Lily gasped. She'd forgotten all about her own magical Friendship Fudge! Archie and Grandma had finished using the scales so Lily carefully measured out the icing sugar.

She made sure to keep checking the

recipe. She didn't want to make any mistakes. The recipe said to stir in the icing sugar a little bit at a time. It turned the mixture thick until it became so thick it was as solid as dough and she couldn't stir any more.

"It's cooled down now, so you can mix the last bit of sugar in with your hands," Grandma told her. "Are they clean?"

Lily held up her hands to show they were very clean. She pushed up her sleeves and began mixing the last of the sugar into the thick fudge mixture with her fingers. She kneaded and squeezed the fudge in her hands.

"I'm putting all my friendliness into the fudge," she told Grandma. "It's going to be perfect."

"So are my cookies," Archie said. He was busy stirring a big bowl of the cookie mixture.

"You can both help decorate the cookies once they're baked," Grandma said. "We can make them look all creepy and scary for Halloween!" Grandma looked into Lily's bowl. "Your fudge looks like it's ready to roll out now," she said. Grandma cleared a space on the table and sprinkled it with icing sugar. "The sugar will stop the fudge sticking to the table."

Lily lifted her fudge mixture from the bowl and plopped it on the table. "This is going to be fun!" She picked up the rolling pin and pushed it down on the lump of fudge

and began to gently roll it out. The fudge mixture smelled sweet and sugary and it looked a delicious chocolatey brown colour. But would it taste magical enough to make Antonia her friend again?

# 5

## Creepy Cookies

Hector meowed loudly as he sat on the kitchen window sill looking out to the garden. "Meeeow," he said again.

"Maybe he's seen a ghost!" Archie said.

Lily looked towards the window. "I can see smoke outside!"

They all hurried over to the window and looked out.

"That's nothing to worry about," said Mum. "It's only Grandpa burning a big pile of leaves."

Orange and yellow and red flames were shooting out of the pile of leaves and the grey smoke was curling up towards the sky.

"It's spooky out there," Archie said, and hurried back to the table.

Lily went back to the table quickly too. Her Friendship Fudge was almost finished! All she had to do now was cut it into little squares. Lily carefully drew straight lines on the rolled-out mixture, then Mum helped by cutting the fudge into little squares.

"You should probably try a piece," Mum suggested. "Just to make sure it's perfect for Antonia."

Lily grinned and bit into one of the little squares. It was delicious! It melted in her mouth, leaving a soft, sweet, creamy taste. "Mmmm."

She offered a piece to Mum and Grandma
and Archie.

"We don't want to eat all your
Friendship Fudge," Mum said. "It's for
Antonia."

"But you're my friends, too," Lily said.

Everyone ate a square of the fudge and
agreed it tasted very special.

"The best I've ever tasted," Grandma
smiled.

"There is a lot of magic in that fudge," Mum said.

"It's so yummy it makes you want to be friendly," Archie grinned.

Lily smiled. It was so nice that Antonia *had* to like it!

She put all the little squares of fudge on to a tray covered in greaseproof paper and put it in the fridge to chill. The Friendship Fudge was done! But Mum, Grandma and Archie were still working hard to get their treats ready.

"Can I help?" Lily asked.

"Yes, please," said Mum. She handed Lily a special baking bag. Inside it was the fluffy white meringue mixture. She showed Lily how to squeeze the mixture out of a nozzle on the end of the bag on to a baking tray to make swirly white ghost shapes. She even added chocolate chip eyes.

"They don't take long to cook, but they
do need a long time to cool," Mum told
them. "So I'll put them in the oven now."

That just left Grandma and Archie's
biscuits still to bake. Grandma had rolled
out the mixture on to the table and

Archie was busy cutting out shapes with the cookie cutters.

"Can you help me, please?" Archie asked Lily.

"Of course," Lily grinned. It looked such fun. She cut out three cats and three witches' hats.

Grandma had greased a baking tray so the biscuits didn't stick and Lily and Archie put all the cookies on it.

The kitchen smelled so lovely and sweet that Lily felt quite tingly. She was sure it was the baking magic working.

As soon as the Meringue Ghosts were ready, Mum took them out of the oven. They were white and plump and crispy with big chocolatey eyes. "I can't wait to taste them," Archie said as Mum set the tray down on the table to cool.

"Can we bake our biscuits now?" Archie asked Grandma. He picked up the tomato-shaped timer. "How long will they take to cook?"

Grandma put the tray of Creepy Cookies in the oven and shut the oven door. "They won't take long."

Lily looked around the busy kitchen.

The meringues were cooling, the biscuits were baking and her fudge was chilling in the fridge.

"Well done, everyone," Grandma said, wiping her hands on her apron.

As Mum washed up, Lily carefully wrote "Friendship Fudge" on the top of the recipe and put it away in her special recipe box in case she ever needed to make it again. Grandma put the magical jar safely back up on the top shelf of the dresser.

Before long, the tomato-shaped timer started to ring. "The biscuits are ready!" Archie said.

Grandma lifted them out of the oven. They smelled delicious. "When they've cooled, you can decorate them," Grandma said. "But there's one thing we've got to do first."

"What?" Lily asked. Just then the

back door opened and Grandpa came in rubbing his tummy.

"Have lunch!" Grandma smiled, getting a delicious-looking plate of sandwiches out of the fridge. They had been so busy that the time had flown by!

Once lunch was over, Grandpa went back into the garden. "What shall we do now?" Lily asked. "Is it time to decorate the cookies?"

"They need to cool down a bit first," Grandma answered. "But it is time for something fun — it's time to change into our Halloween costumes!"

Lily gasped. She didn't have a costume! "But what will I wear?" she wailed.

Mum smiled. "Don't worry," she said. "I brought your cat costume from last year along just in case you changed your mind." Mum opened a carrier bag and held up a black cat costume. There was a black leotard, a headband with ears on, a long swishy tail and black gloves.

Lily was delighted. "Thanks, Mum! I'm going to be a cat like Hector!"

"I'm so glad you're coming to the party," Mum said.

"And me," said Archie.

"We all are," said Grandma.

Archie was growing more and more excited. "I can't wait! I can't wait!" he kept saying. He was jumping up and down so fast that his spider costume legs were flying around everywhere.

Mum and Grandma laughed and Lily smiled, too. Halloween was going to be fun after all. She was going to the party *and* she had a costume to wear!

Lily ran upstairs to Grandma's yellow bedroom to get changed into her costume.

Hector scampered up the stairs after her and sat on the floor watching as Lily turned into a cat. He looked very puzzled.

His eyes were wide and his ears were sticking up, just like the ears on Lily's costume.

Lily caught sight of herself in the mirror and laughed. "I look just like you, Hector!" she grinned. "Except I'm a black Halloween cat and you're orange and stripy. And something's missing. . ." She went out on to the landing and called down the stairs.

"Mum? I need whiskers!"

Mum came upstairs carrying a bag. Inside it was a box of face paints. She painted a set of whiskers on Lily's face that went all the way across her cheeks and then she gave her a black nose.

"What about me?" Archie asked as he scurried into the room. "My face needs painting, too!"

"Hmmmm," said Mum. "What kind of spider are you?"

"A spooky spider," Archie said.

Mum gave him a white face with two big black spider eyes and two long fangs. Archie looked in the mirror. "I look scary!" he said with a huge grin.

"What costume are you wearing, Mum?" Lily asked.

"I'm going as a mummy, of course!" Mum said, pulling rolls of toilet paper from the bag. "Can you help me?"

"I'll wrap your legs!" Lily said.

"I'll do your arms," said Archie.

They giggled and laughed as they wrapped Mum in the paper. She looked very funny, but not really very scary.

"Lily? Archie?" Grandma called as they wrapped the last of the paper around Mum's middle. "It's time to ice the cookies!"

Lily and Archie rushed downstairs.

But as they got to the bottom of the stairs, they suddenly stopped and stared. Archie gave a shocked gasp and grabbed Lily's hand. There was a witch in the kitchen!

# 6

## Monsters in the House

"Do you like my hat?" the witch asked. Her black pointed hat was decorated with silver stars and moons.

Lily blinked. "Grandma? Is that you?"

The witch laughed. "Yes, it's me!"

Lily and Archie giggled as Grandma did a twirl. Her long black dress and cloak swirled and swished across the floor. She also had a magic wand that she waved around in the air. "I'm going to cast a spell," she said. "Widdy, waddy, woodee woo! Look what I have wished for you!"

Grandma pointed the wand at the table. As if by magic there were lots of tubes of coloured icing out ready to decorate the Creepy Cookies.

"Hurrah!" Archie said. He clambered up on a chair at the table and picked up a tube of black icing. "I'm going to put scary eyes on the pumpkin cookies. And sharp teeth, too!"

Lily looked at all the tubes of icing. "I'm going to give the cookie cats white whiskers and green eyes," she laughed.

Lily and Archie had so much fun drizzling the icing over the cookies.

"Oops!" said Archie as a cookie broke in his hands.

"You'd better eat that one," Mum smiled.

Archie grinned and gave one of the pieces to Lily. The cookie was crunchy and crumbly and the icing was sweet in her mouth. "Mmmmmm," she said and licked her lips.

"Creepy Cookies are yummy!" Archie agreed.

When the cookies were all decorated and the icing had set, Grandma and Mum carefully packed them into boxes along with the Meringue Ghosts. All that had to be done then was for Lily to arrange her fudge inside the red gift box. Grandma added a piece of pink ribbon and tied it in a bow.

"Thank you, Grandma. It looks lovely!" Lily told her. She crossed her fingers tightly. Antonia had to like it!

Archie was crawling around the floor being a spider. "Can we go to the party now?"

"Yes, I think it's time to go," Mum agreed. "But we need to say goodbye to Grandpa."

Archie waved Grandma's witch's wand and pointed it at the door. "I wish, I wish, Grandpa was here," he said.

As if by magic, the back door swung open and in walked Grandpa. He was carrying an enormous pumpkin. A cold draught blew through the kitchen as he shut the door. When he saw them all in their Halloween costumes he took a step back and pretended to be shocked. "There are monsters in the house!"

"Don't be scared, Grandpa," Archie laughed. "It's just us!"

Lily ran over to greet him. "Oh, Grandpa!" she said. "You've carved a pumpkin!"

"So that's what you've been doing in the shed," Grandma smiled.

Grandpa held up the pumpkin. Its round spooky face had two big staring eyes, a triangular nose and a wide mouth with sharp teeth.

"Let's light the candle inside the pumpkin," Grandpa said. "Then we can see its face glow in the dark."

He set the pumpkin down on the table and lit the candle. Grandma switched off the kitchen lights and the room turned dark, except for the candle that flickered and burned, turning the pumpkin eyes and mouth into a flaming orange glow. It was so bright it lit up all their faces.

Archie looked around the darkened kitchen. "It's spooooooooooky in here!" he whispered to Lily, trying to scare her. But just then the cuckoo clock called, "Cuckoo! Cuckoo!" and Archie was the one who jumped with fright. Everyone laughed.

Mum gave Archie a hug. "The cuckoo clock is telling us it's time for the party!"

"Let me take your photograph before you go!" Grandpa said. They all crowded around the pumpkin. Lily picked up Hector and they all smiled.

"Click!" went the camera and the photograph was taken.

It was time to leave. Lily suddenly felt very nervous. She looked up at the magic jar and wished as hard as she could that the baking magic would work again.

# 7

## Party Time

Lily sat quietly in the back seat of the car holding the little red box of Friendship Fudge. It was already dark outside, and as they drove along the streets, Archie pointed to glowing pumpkins in windows and people in their fancy dress costumes setting off for Halloween parties. His spider legs kept landing on Lily's shoulder and across her face but she didn't mind. She was too busy making sure her special box of Friendship Fudge didn't get squashed.

When the car pulled up at the kerb outside Antonia's house, Lily looked up at the brightly lit pumpkins on the step outside the front door and the orange and black balloons on the garden gate.

"I'm going to like this party," Archie said as Mum helped him out of the car. Lily watched him run up the steps with his spider legs waving around. He had to stand on his tiptoes to ring the doorbell. "Come on, Lily!" he called, but Lily didn't want to go into the house without Mum and Grandma. She stood on the pavement and waited while they unpacked the plastic tubs of treats from the boot of the car. Lily could hear laughter and music inside the house. It sounded as if everyone was having a lovely time.

Antonia's mum opened the door. She was dressed as a witch, too. But her hat was floppy, her cheeks were rosy and she was smiling.

"I'm so glad you could all come!" She saw the boxes of treats Mum and Grandma were carrying. "Thank you so much for helping."

Inside, the party was noisy and exciting. Everywhere Lily looked there were witches and angels and fairies and goblins all dashing around.

Grandma and Mum quickly got to work, setting the treats out on the long party table in the kitchen. Lots of people from Lily's class gathered round as Mum put her Meringue Ghosts on a plate.

"They look yummy!" a pirate said.

Archie helped set out the Creepy Cookies.

"Can we eat them now?" a skeleton asked. "I'm starving."

Antonia's mum said they would have to

wait just a little longer until it was time for tea.

"Hello, Lily!" said two green-faced monsters. It was the twins from Lily's class, Bella and Freya.

Then Eve came rushing towards her dressed as a bat. "Help!" she giggled. "I'm being chased by a vampire!"

The vampire had a very white face and long plastic fangs. He raced by with his purple and red cloak flapping. "Hi, Lily!" he said.

"Hi, Sam," Lily said.

All the class were there in fancy dress. There were ghosts and witches and bats and spiders, but there was no sign of Antonia anywhere.

Just then, Lily spotted Antonia's little dog, Mozzie, sitting on the floor, staring up at someone dressed as a pumpkin.

The pumpkin was wearing black tap dance shoes. It must be Antonia!

Lily felt very nervous. She didn't know what to say to Antonia. But then Mozzie came trotting over to say hello. Lily kneeled down to pat his little head. His soft nose started sniffing the box of fudge Lily was carrying. "It's not for you!" Lily laughed. "It's for Antonia."

"Hello, Lily," Antonia said shyly.

Lily stood up. Antonia had walked over and was now standing next to her.

"Hello," Lily said.

"I like your costume," Antonia said.

Lily tried to smile. "I like yours, too." She held out the little red gift box. "I've brought you a present."

Antonia looked at the red box with the pink ribbon. "Thank you!" She opened it and looked inside. "Fudge!" She gave

an even bigger smile. "My favourite!" She popped a square in her mouth.

Lily crossed her fingers and hoped the baking magic worked. It had always worked before. . .

"Mmmmm," Antonia said as she ate the fudge. Her eyes were sparkling. *That must be the magic working*, Lily told herself.

Antonia licked her lips. "It's delicious!" she gasped. She gave Lily a big friendly smile. "Can I have another piece, please?"

"Yes," Lily told her. "I made it *all* for you." She gave a shy smile. "It's called Friendship Fudge."

"Friendship Fudge?" Antonia asked. She looked sad. "So why did you stop being my friend? And why didn't you want to come to my party?"

Lily was confused. "But I thought *you* didn't want to be *my* friend and that's why you didn't invite me to your party."

Antonia shook her head. "I *did* invite you to my party. I invited you first of all! I put the invitation on your desk."

Lily shook her head. Then she gasped. "It must have got lost in the mess! My desk was so

untidy I didn't see it!" Grandma was right.
It had all been a big misunderstanding!
"I must have put the invitation in the
bin with the scrap bits of paper from my
Halloween mask!"

"It doesn't matter," Antonia said softly.
"You're here now. Please can we be
friends again?"

Lily nodded. Even Mozzie was jumping
up and down and barking. She was
so happy. But just then Stephie came
hurrying over and stood beside
Antonia. She was dressed as a zombie.

"Antonia? Did you show Lily what you
bought today?" she asked.

Lily remembered seeing them that
morning from the car window and tried
very hard not to feel jealous as Antonia
took a tiny box from her pocket and
handed it to Lily.

"I helped her choose it," Stephie said.

Lily felt her stomach churn. She was glad she and Antonia were friends again, but was Stephie her *best* friend now? Lily opened the box. Inside it was a little bracelet made of tiny coloured beads.

"It's a friendship bracelet," Antonia explained. "Do you like it?"

Lily liked it a lot. "It's lovely," she said and handed it back to Antonia.

"But it's for you!" Stephie said. "Antonia bought it so you won't fight ever again! So you can always be best friends!"

Antonia nodded.

Lily gave a big smile. So Antonia did want to be best friends. The magical Friendship Fudge had worked and her wish had come true!

Lily put the little bracelet on her wrist.

It glittered and shone in the party lights. "Thank you," Lily said.

"Thank you for making me extra special Friendship Fudge!" Antonia grinned at her.

Lily looked at the little red box of Friendship Fudge. Then she turned to Stephie. "Would you like a piece?" she asked, holding out the box.

"Yes, please!" Stephie grinned.

Just then Grandma came over to join them. "Did it work?" she whispered to Lily.

Lily nodded happily. "And I think I've made a new friend too!"

Grandma gave a big smile. "Time for tea, everyone!" she announced.

Stephie squealed with delight and hurried through to the kitchen along with all the other witches and ghosts and skeletons and bats.

Antonia and Lily held hands and hurried through for tea. Archie was already munching one of his Creepy Cookies and Lily and Antonia's mums were making sure everyone had enough to eat.

Antonia held up the little red box to show her mum. "Look what Lily made especially for me. It's called Friendship Fudge."

"It looks delicious," Antonia's mum said. She smiled at Lily. "And thank you for helping Grandma and Mum to make such nice treats for our party."

"That's what friends are for," Lily said.

Everyone was smiling and laughing and tucking into the delicious food. She was so glad she had helped make the treats after all. Now it was time to enjoy the party with her best friend! And Antonia was right. It really was going to be the best Halloween party ever!

Look out for more **Bake a Wish** books

Bake a Wish

Get-Better Jelly

Includes FANTASTIC cut-out-and-keep recipe card!

Lorna Ho...

Bake a Wish

Feel Fearless Flapjacks

Includes FANTASTIC cut-out-and-keep recipe card!

Lo...

Bake a Wish

Mend-It Muffins

Includes FANTASTIC cut-out-and-keep recipe card!

Lorna Honeywell